Good Night, ARCTIC

Good Night, Arctic: A Dreamy Bedtime Story with Gentle Goodnight Rhymes for Toddlers and Children

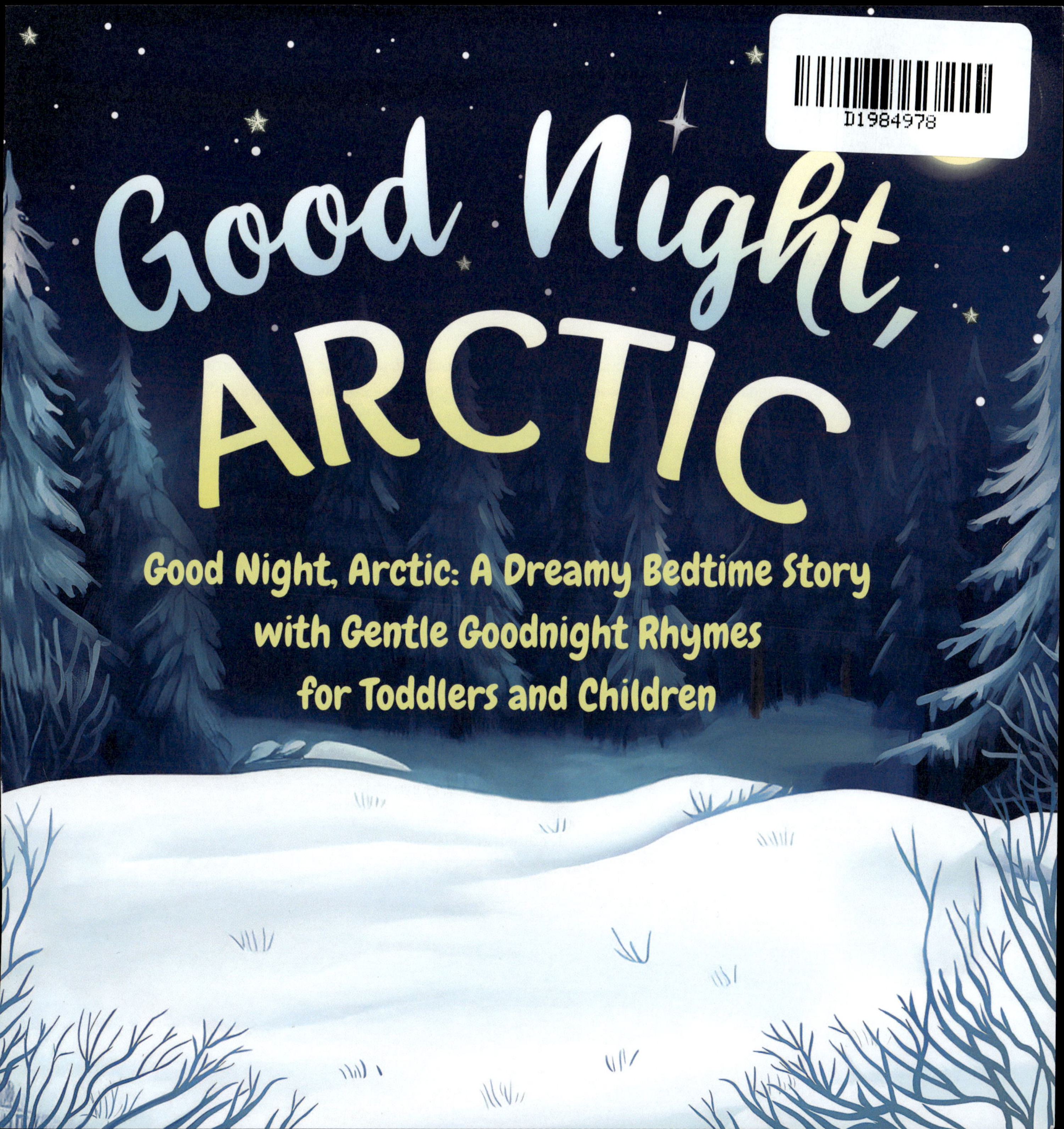

Good Night, Arctic:
A Dreamy Bedtime Story with Gentle Goodnight Rhymes for Toddlers and Children

Threeglav is represented by:
Sontig Media GmbH
Saarweg 16
53129 Bonn
Germany

Production and publishing by Sontig Media GmbH
Edited by Michelle Roberts
Cover and interior design by Rejenne Pavon-Mendoza

1. edition 2025
ISBN 978-3-9825543-6-5

This book belongs to:

As the snow glows faintly
in the fading light,
Arctic animals prepare
for the calm of night.

The night feels near,
the cold winds hum.
Arctic Weasel wonders
when the moon will come.

Penguin rests tiredly
by the water so near.
She closes her eyes
as the bright stars appear.

Polar Bear falls asleep
under aurora's light.
The colors dance gently,
waving goodnight.

Caribou curls up
in the forest so deep.
In the frosty night air,
she falls fast asleep.

Walrus stretches out
on the icy shore,
dreaming of adventures
and places to explore.

The stars are sparkling,
quiet and high.
The polar Fox whispers,
“Goodnight, sky.”

As the chilly night whispers,
so soft and so deep,
Ptarmigan sighs gently,
ready for sleep.

Arctic Hare sleeps
in a blanket of snow,
as the moon shines softly
with its gentle glow.

The full moon beams
in the quiet sky.
Tundra Swan gazes,
her thoughts floating by.

Puffin rests by the water,
so calm and so deep,
thinking of the day
before drifting off to sleep.

In the gentle waves
that softly play,
Beluga Whale drifts,
tired from his day.

As Snowy Owl perches
on a branch so high,
the full moon watches
from the quiet sky.

The earth feels cold
under the starry sky.
A Musk Ox pauses,
letting time pass by.

The sea is calm,
the waves softly play.
Seal closes her eyes,
ending her day.

The moon watches
over the forest so deep,
as Lynx curls up happily,
content in his sleep.

The snowy ground stretches
under the moon's glowing light.
An Arctic Lemming watches,
eyes sleepy but bright.

The Arctic Wolf rests,
the world feels slow,
calm in the stillness
of the falling snow.

The stars twinkle softly,
the night feels deep.
The Arctic is quiet,
its animals are all asleep.

Printed in Germany
by Amazon Distribution
GmbH, Erfurt

10312146R00026